YOKO'S
World of Kindness

YOKO'S WORLD OF KINDNESS

 ## GOLDEN RULES FOR A HAPPY CLASSROOM

ROSEMARY WELLS

Interior Illustrations by

JOHN NEZ *and* JODY WHEELER

HYPERION BOOKS FOR CHILDREN
NEW YORK

First collected edition

10 9 8 7 6 5 4 3 2 1

Printed in Singapore

Library of Congress Cataloging-in-Publication Data on file.

Reinforced binding

ISBN 0-7868-5109-0

Visit www.hyperionbooksforchildren.com

Contents

Mama, Don't Go!

GOLDEN RULE THE FIRST

It is not easy to say good-bye.
But the one who loves us always comes back.

Yoko could not wait for the first day of school. She wanted to say hello to lots of new friends. She wanted to learn all the words to all the songs. She wanted to play with the beautiful silver beads in Mrs. Jenkins's classroom.

But Yoko did not want her mother to leave.

On Monday morning, Yoko's mother stayed
for ten minutes after school began.

But when Yoko's mother put on her coat,
Yoko cried loud and hard. Everyone got upset.

So Yoko's mother sat in the back of the classroom for the whole morning.

On Tuesday morning, Yoko wanted to string a necklace of colored beads.

She could not wait to write ABCDEFG on the blackboard. But she was still not ready to have her mother leave.

Yoko's mother said, "Yoko, I have to go home. I have work to do."

"Oh, no," said Yoko. "If you leave, I will cry so much, everybody will get upset again."

So Yoko's mother could not leave.

After the alphabet song, Yoko's mother was thirsty. "I am going to the cafeteria for a drink of apple juice," said Yoko's mother.

"Yes, but come right back," said Yoko.

"I will come right back," said Yoko's mother.

Yoko waited for her mother to come back.

In ten minutes, her mother came back.

"Now may I leave for an hour?" asked Yoko's mother.

"No," said Yoko. "I am not ready for you to leave again."

On Wednesday morning, Yoko wanted to hear story time. She sang the "Falling Leaves" song with her new friend, Timothy. But Yoko was still not ready for her mother to leave.

At snack time, Mrs. Jenkins said, "Oh, my goodness! We are out of celery sticks and crackers. We can't have snack time with nothing to eat. Yoko, will you let me ask your mother to go to the store?"

Yoko turned around. "How long will it take?"
she asked.

"Maybe fifteen minutes. Maybe twenty,"
said Yoko's mother.

Yoko watched her mother drive away. She stayed at the window until her mother came back. But she did not cry.

"Why do you worry so much about your mother, Yoko?" asked Timothy.

"Because I don't want her to leave me," said Yoko.

"But she will always come back," said Timothy.

"I still feel afraid," said Yoko.

"Oh, mothers always come back," said
Timothy. "They just come back and come back,
and after a while, you have to ask them to stay
home."

"Ask them to stay home!" said Yoko. "I could never do that."

"I like to surprise my mother," said Timothy.

"Surprise her?" asked Yoko.

"I think you should give your mother a day off," said Timothy. "Everyone needs a day off."

On Thursday, Yoko could not wait to feed the goldfish.

She could not wait to sing "The Star-Spangled Banner" with Nora and Fritz. But Yoko was not ready for her mother to leave.

"Do we have any birthdays today?" asked Mrs. Jenkins.

Nobody raised a hand.

"Are you sure?" asked Mrs. Jenkins.

Nobody raised a hand.

Then, from the back of the classroom, Yoko's mother raised her hand.

"It's my birthday today," said Yoko's mother.

"Oh, well!" said Mrs. Jenkins. "We have to do something special."

Mrs. Jenkins asked Yoko to come up to the front of the class.

She whispered something in Yoko's ear.

Yoko whispered back.

Mrs. Jenkins whispered back to Yoko.

And Yoko nodded her head.

Then Yoko ran back to her mother.

"You have to leave now, Mama," said Yoko.

"We're going to make a surprise for you."

So Yoko's mother had to leave.

Yoko watched her drive the car away.

"She'll come back," said Timothy. "They always do."

Yoko's mother came back at the end of the day.

The class had made a cake. They made hats with sparkles, and everyone sang, "Happy Birthday, Yoko's mama!"

Yoko went home with her mother.

They had their hats and their bead necklaces and extra pieces of birthday cake.

"That was a wonderful surprise!" said Yoko's mother.

"Yes, it was," said Yoko, "but the best surprise of all is yet to come!"

"What is it?" asked Yoko's mother.

"It's a surprise!" said Yoko.

Yoko waited until the next morning to
surprise her mother.

"Here it is!" said Yoko.

"I can't see it!"
said Yoko's mother.

"That's because it is
a day off!" said Yoko.

"A day off!" said Yoko's mother.

"You may do whatever you want today,"
said Yoko.

So Yoko's mother did whatever she wanted.

And at three o'clock, Yoko watched her mother's car come up the school driveway.

"There she is!" said Timothy.

"They always come back," said Yoko.

"Next week you'll have to ask her to stay home!" said Timothy.

"Yes, I will!" said Yoko.

Doris's Dinosaur

GOLDEN RULE THE SECOND

*Many great geniuses are thought to be crazy
because they are different.
Never criticize the creations of another
person's heart and mind.*

Yoko

grace

claude

HAZEL

Doris

LILY

"What are we studying, boys and girls?" asked Mrs. Jenkins.

"Dinosaurs!" answered everybody.

"Yes!" said Mrs. Jenkins. "Now it is time to decorate the halls of Hilltop School with our paintings of dinosaurs.

"Try and paint the best dinosaur you can.
You may pick out any kind you like—
flying, walking, or swimming."

Grace chose a pterodactyl. She copied it perfectly from the encyclopedia. It was fabulous.

Claude's apatosaurus was wonderful.

Yoko finished her stegosaurus early and helped one of the Frank twins with his painting of a flying raptor. Everybody chose a wonderful dinosaur.

"Doris, how about yours?" asked Mrs. Jenkins.

"I can't," said Doris.

"Let me help," offered Grace.

"I don't want help," said Doris.

Doris dipped her paintbrush into the blue color.
She swirled it on the paper. Then Doris dipped
her blue brush in the yellow paint. It turned green.

She painted green blobs.

After that, Doris put down her brush in disgust.

"See!" said Doris
with a snort. "I can't
paint!"

Everyone noticed
Doris's painting,
but no one said
anything about it.

Mrs. Jenkins hung all the pictures in the hallway of Hilltop School.

Everyone admired them.

But Doris knew everyone hated her painting.
"Doris," said Mrs. Jenkins, "you don't have to
paint anything you don't want to."

But Doris knew everyone laughed at her because she could not paint a dinosaur. If Doris found someone looking too hard at her blue swirl, she thwacked her tail loudly on the floor to scare them away.

One day during playtime, Doris came inside for a drink of water. Charles was staring at Doris's blue swirl. He was smiling.

"What are you looking at?" asked Doris.

"I am looking at your painting," said Charles.

"Why? Why are you looking?" asked Doris.

"I like it," said Charles.

"I don't believe you!" said Doris.

"No, really, I like it," said Charles. "This picture makes me feel all peaceful inside."

"You're crazy!" said Doris.

But every day before rest time, Charles stood in the hall and looked at Doris's picture. Charles sighed, and then closed his eyes.

"Charles seems to like your picture, Doris," said Mrs. Jenkins.

"He's crazy," said Doris.

"Oh, I don't think so," said Mrs. Jenkins. "Now, what are we doing tomorrow, class?"

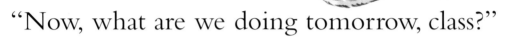

"We are going to the museum to see the dinosaurs!" said everyone.

"That's right," said Mrs. Jenkins. "Remember to bring your dinosaur notebooks, one dollar spending money, and your lunch."

Mr. Ossio showed everybody around the museum. In the first room were the bones of a very old woolly mammoth.

"Is a woolly mammoth a dinosaur, boys and girls?" asked Mr. Ossio.

"No!" answered everyone.

"Why not?" asked Mr. Ossio.

"Because a woolly mammoth is a mammal!" answered almost everyone.

"What a smart class with a good teacher!"
said Mr. Ossio.

"Take out your notebooks, class," said Mrs. Jenkins.

Timothy drew a hundred-toothed rattlesnake.

Yoko drew a pincher turtle.

"What's your picture, Doris?" asked Grace.

"I can't draw," said Doris.

"Let me show you how," said Grace.

Grace showed Doris how to draw a woolly mammoth.

After Grace left, Doris colored her whole page with her red marker. Then she put little black dots in the middle.

Yoko looked at it. She said nothing.

"You think I am stupid," said Doris.

Soon it was time for lunch.

Lunch was in the garden.

Mrs. Jenkins began to count heads.

She could not find Charles.

"Charles, where are you?"

Mrs. Jenkins called.

Charles did not come.

"Everyone!" said Mrs. Jenkins. "Please put down your sandwiches and find Charles."

Claude found him.

"Where were you?" asked Mrs. Jenkins.

"I was in the other part of the museum,"

said Charles. "Come see!"

Everyone ate their sandwiches and
followed Charles. Mr. Ossio was the guide.

"Oooh!" said everyone.

"What are these?" asked Grace.

"These are paintings by one of the most wonderful artists in the world," said Mr. Ossio. "The artist's name was Henri Matisse."

Everybody stared. There on the far wall was a blue swirl. On the right wall was a red square with little black dots.

"What do you think about these pictures, boys and girls?" asked Mr. Ossio.

For a long, long time nobody answered.

Then Doris's hand went up.

"What do you think, young lady?" asked Mr. Ossio.

"I guess Mr. Matisse didn't feel like drawing dinosaurs," said Doris.

On the bus ride home, everyone noticed that Doris was smiling the whole way.

Bubble-Gum Radar

GOLDEN RULE THE THIRD

Teasing hurts like hitting.
It always goes under the guise of joking.

"It's Square-Dance Day!" said Mrs. Jenkins.

"Hooray!" shouted everyone.

"Hooray!" shouted the Franks, louder than everyone else.

The Franks spit their bubble gum into the air over Nora's head.

It came down and hit her in the ear.

"Ouch!" yelled Nora.

"We were just playing around," said the Franks.

Mrs. Jenkins did not even turn around from the blackboard.

"My bubble-gum radar is beeping!" she said.

"Please take the gum out. No gum in school!"

"Timothy, would you like to come up?" asked Mrs. Jenkins. "Please draw the class a square."

Timothy went to the blackboard. He drew a triangle. Then he sat down.

"That's a wonderful triangle, Timothy," said Mrs. Jenkins. "One more side, and it's a square. Try again, Timothy."

Timothy tried to get up from his seat. He was stuck.

There was a big piece of pink bubble gum on Timothy's chair.

"Who put the gum on Timothy's seat?" asked Mrs. Jenkins.

No one answered.

"My bubble-gum radar tells me it might be

someone whose name is Frank," said Mrs. Jenkins.

"We were just kidding," said one Frank.

"We didn't know he'd sit down on it," said the other Frank.

"The gum goes in the wastebasket," said Mrs. Jenkins. "All of it, please."

"Doris, will you come up and show the class how many corners there are in a square?" asked Mrs. Jenkins.

Doris went to the board.

Doris tried to decide where the corners for the square were. Then she thwacked her big tail on the floor.

At that moment, both Franks began to make
rude noises with their hands under their armpits.

"That will be enough, Franks," said
Mrs. Jenkins.

In science class, Fritz was ready to show his experiment. He poured baking soda into the cone of his volcano.

"You think you are so smart!" said one of the Franks. He pushed Fritz's volcano. The volcano fell over.

"Be careful, please!" cried Fritz. "Now I have to put the volcano together all over again."

"Just kidding!" said Frank.

"I think Frank will have to wait in the quiet corner for a while," said Mrs. Jenkins.

Frank had to sit in the Quiet Corner during playtime.

On the playground, the other Frank ran for a football pass.

"Get out of my way!" he shouted.

Nora was playing hopscotch. Frank banged right into Nora.

He did not say he was sorry. Instead he said, "Just kidding!"

Yoko helped Nora up. "You have a nosebleed," said Yoko. "I will take you to the school nurse."

The school nurse asked Nora to lie down.

She put an ice pack on Nora's nose.

"You'll feel better right away, Nora," she said.

"Did somebody bump into you?" she asked.

Nora and Yoko were quiet.

"I bet it was one of those Franks," said the school nurse.

Mrs. Jenkins had seen everything through the classroom window. When playtime was over, both Franks were sitting in the Quiet Corner.

"Now, do you think you can eat lunch without bothering anybody else?" asked Mrs. Jenkins.

"Oh sure!" said one Frank.

"We were just kidding, anyway," said the other Frank.

But during lunchtime, when Mrs. Jenkins was not looking, one Frank sat on Claude's sandwich.

The other Frank squirted Doris's squeeze cheese out the window.

"We were just kidding!" they said to Doris and Claude.

"It's square-dance practice time!" said Mrs. Jenkins.

"I want everybody to pick their partner."

Yoko picked Timothy,

 Charles picked Nora.

Grace picked Claude.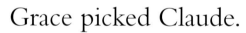

Doris picked Fritz.

But no one picked the Franks.

"No fair!" the Franks complained. "No fun!"

"Well, you can't square-dance without a partner," said Mrs. Jenkins.

"But nobody picked us!" said the Franks.

"You can pick each other!" said Mrs. Jenkins.

"No way am I going to pick him!"
said one Frank.

"Why not?" asked Mrs. Jenkins.

"He sneezes on me and steps on my feet,"
said one Frank.

"He pushes!" said the other Frank. "And he pops his gum."

"And today you have both been mean to everyone!" said Grace.

Mrs. Jenkins sat down at the piano. "Everybody stop and sing the 'Friendly' song!" she said.

Everybody sang,

"Be my pal.

See me smile!

Wear my shoes

And walk a mile.

Hold my hand

Be my friend.

And we'll never never never never

never NEVER fight again!"

The Franks picked each other.

Everybody squared-danced.

And Mrs. Jenkins's bubble-gum radar didn't beep once.

The
Secret Birthday

GOLDEN RULE THE FOURTH

Don't whisper about who is in and who is out.
It is hurtful and unkind.

On Monday morning, Noisy Nora did not say hello on the school bus.

She did not say anything.

"She looks as if she's got a whole bag of nuts in her mouth," said Timothy.

"What's in your mouth, Nora?" asked Yoko.

"Nfng," said Nora.

"Something's in your mouth," said Timothy.

"Scrt," said Nora.

Nora would not open her mouth. She would not open her mouth during the "Good Morning" song.

She did not open
her mouth during
show-and-tell.
All she would say
was "Bmf!"

"Something is
very wrong with Nora," said Mrs. Jenkins.

"Nora, perhaps you can tell me about it at
lunchtime."

At lunchtime,
Mrs. Jenkins took Nora
to the Quiet Corner.
"What on earth is in
your mouth, Nora?"
she asked.

Nora blurted it out. "A secret!" she said.

"Oh! A secret!" said Mrs. Jenkins.

"I can't tell," said Nora.

"Well, if it is a secret, I will not ask about it," said Mrs. Jenkins.

"It's about my birthday!" said Nora.

"Your birthday?" said Mrs. Jenkins.

"Yes. My birthday party. My mama says our house is too small for a big party, so I can only have five guests."

"Oh, dear," said Mrs. Jenkins.

"Yes! And I'm not allowed to tell anyone! You said, No birthday talk at school, so I can't say anything!"

"That's the rule!" said Mrs. Jenkins.

"But I don't know who can come to the party or not!" said Nora.

"Mama put the invitations in the mailbox today. I will not know who is coming for three more days!"

"Good things are worth waiting for,"
said Mrs. Jenkins.

"Yes, but I don't want to wait," said Nora.
"I want to find out who is coming, right now!"

"You are not allowed to do that in school,
Nora," said Mrs. Jenkins. "If you do, somebody's
feelings are going to be hurt."

"That's why I have to keep it in!" said Nora.

"Well, maybe you don't have to keep the
secret right in your mouth," said Mrs. Jenkins.

"Yes, I do!"
said Nora.

Nora kept her birthday secret right inside her mouth for three more days, until just before playtime. She did not see Grace hiding in the girls' room.

"Are you coming to my party?" Nora whispered to Yoko.

"Yes! Who else is coming?" whispered Yoko back.

"Timothy, Charles, Claude, and Fritz," said Nora.

Grace waited for Yoko and Nora to go out to the playground.

"No fair!" said Grace when she spotted Doris by the cubbies.

"What is no fair?" asked Doris.

"We are NOT invited to Nora's birthday party!" said Grace.

"And it's mean and no fair. See if I invite her to my party!"

Doris thwacked her tail.

Out on the playground, the Franks came running.

"What's up?" asked the Franks.

"Nora's having a party. We're not invited," said Doris.

Grace added, "I'm telling Mrs. Jenkins that Nora talked birthday talk in school and hurt all our feelings!"

Grace waited until everyone was playing happily.

Then she sat down and sulked.

"What's the matter, Grace?" asked Mrs. Jenkins.

"My feelings are hurt," said Grace.

"What happened?" asked Mrs. Jenkins.

"Nora talked birthday talk, and we are left
out!" said Grace.

"I believe you might be talking more birthday
talk than Nora, Grace," said Mrs. Jenkins.

"Not true! No fair!" said Grace.

On the school bus, Grace and the Franks and Doris sang "We're not invited and we don't care!" all the way home.

In her seat, Nora tried to shrink herself down to the size of a pea.

"I don't want to have any birthday party at all," said Nora to her mother.

"Why ever not?" asked Nora's mother.

"I'm running away from all of this forever," said Nora.

"Be back in time for supper," said her mother.

The next morning, Nora was the first one on the school bus. Henry, the bus driver, said, "Good morning, Nora! You do not look happy. What is the matter?"

"Everybody hates me," said Nora in a grumpy voice.

"Everybody hates you!" said Henry. "Why on earth would that be?"

Nora did not answer. She glared out the window. The school bus passed the children's hospital.

"I would rather be in the children's hospital with two broken legs than have everybody hate me," said Nora.

"Fiddle-dee-dee!" said Henry. "I go in there all the time. I help out with the kids. Believe me, you would not want to have two broken legs and be in the hospital, Nora."

"Do they have birthdays there?" asked Nora.

"Everybody has birthdays," said Henry. "Even in the hospital. They have a big cafeteria."

Nora had an idea. After the "Good Morning" song, she told her idea to Mrs. Jenkins.

Mrs. Jenkins asked the class for volunteers.

"We are having a secret birthday!" she said. "No one will know where it is or who it is for! Nobody will be left out!"

Saturday at lunchtime, Henry jumped into his school bus. The gears squeaked, and the bus lurched onto the road. First he picked up Nora and her mother. They had birthday cakes.

Then he picked up Timothy.

 Timothy had fifteen
bags of chips.

Claude was next.
He had jelly beans.

Yoko's mother had made special sushi.

Charles brought ice cream.

Fritz had chocolate sauce.

Doris lugged squeeze

cheese and crackers.

The Franks' dad had cooked up a pot

of franks and beans.

The last stop was Grace's house. Grace's mother helped her get thirty sandwiches onto the bus.

"Where are we going?" asked everybody, but Henry wouldn't tell.

The bus stopped outside a building where no one had ever been before.

"Where are we?" asked Fritz.

"It's the children's hospital," said Claude.
"I can read the sign. There is Mrs. Jenkins!"

The party was a great success. When it was over, all the patients in the hospital felt much better.

And so did Nora.

The
School Play

GOLDEN RULE THE FIFTH

We cannot all be most important at the same minute.
Sooner or later we all get a turn.

"Good morning, boys and girls!"
said Mrs. Jenkins.

"Good morning, Mrs. Jenkins!" said everyone.

Everyone held hands in a circle and sang the
"Good Morning" song.

"Good morning on my left!

Good morning on my right!

May our day be filled with play

Until the stars come out tonight!"

"Today, boys and girls," said Mrs. Jenkins, "we will choose the roles for our class play!"

"I want to be the queen!" said Doris.

"We're going to be Frankenstein!" said the Franks.

"There is no queen and no Frankenstein in this play," said Mrs. Jenkins. "Our play is about keeping our teeth strong and clean. Now, who wants to play the part of the dentist?"

Claude raised his hand and said, "Me! Me! Me!"

Timothy got to be the toothbrush.

Doris was the dental floss. Nora was the

toothpaste.

Grace was the bottle of mouthwash. One Frank was a Caramel Clump Chocolate Bar. The other Frank was a wisdom tooth. And Yoko was a cavity.

Everyone went home learning the lines for the play. Everyone went home happy, except Yoko.

Yoko played her violin. But the music sounded so sad that her mother asked, "What's the matter, my little cherry blossom?"

"I am only a cavity in the school play," said
Yoko.

"Surely the cavity does something interesting,"
said Yoko's mother.

"No," said Yoko.

"The cavity just sits there. Then the Caramel Clump Chocolate Bar gets on top and says, 'I am stuck here forever!' After that, the dentist puts a filling in me."

"Well, I will make you the best cavity costume anyone has ever seen," said Yoko's mother.

At play practice, the class chairs were set in a half circle. "They look like a mouth full of teeth," said Timothy.

Yoko asked Nora if she would like to trade being the toothpaste for being a cavity.

"No," said Nora. "I don't want to be an old cavity. The cavity doesn't say a word!"

Claude wouldn't trade, either. Neither would Doris or Grace or anyone else. No one wanted to be the cavity.

"Come, Yoko," said Mrs. Jenkins, "time to sit in your chair. Claude, are you ready to put in the filling?"

"I am ready," said Claude.

"What do you have behind your back, Claude?" asked Mrs. Jenkins.

"It's my father's drill," said Claude. "It makes a perfect noise."

"You can't use tools in the play, Claude," said Mrs. Jenkins. "I am sure you can make excellent drill noises by yourself."

"It's no fun to be the dentist if I can't use my drill," said Claude.

"If we use our imaginations, we can all be happy with our parts in the play," said Mrs. Jenkins.

Every morning, Mrs. Jenkins called a play practice.

Every morning, Claude complained.

"I don't want to make buzzing noises. I want to use my father's drill," said Claude.

Thursday afternoon, on the school bus,

Timothy said, "You look unhappy, Yoko."

"I don't like being an old cavity," said Yoko.

"Who would?" said Timothy.

"What's in the suitcase?" Timothy asked.

"My violin," said Yoko.

"Can I see it?" Timothy asked.

Yoko showed him.

"Can I try it?"

Yoko let him.

But she had to put her hands over her ears.

"Stop that noise!" said everyone on the bus.

"You know what?" asked Timothy.

"What?" said Yoko.

"The violin sounds just like a dentist's drill!"
Timothy plucked the strings.

"I love it! I want to do it again!" he said.

"I have an idea," said Yoko.

Yoko and her mother made her cavity costume.
Yoko painted a box black. Yoko's mother made
a white tooth top.

On Friday morning, all the mamas and
daddies came to the school and sat in their seats.

The curtain opened.

The play began. Timothy came out holding his toothbrush.

He dipped into Nora's toothpaste and brushed
every tooth up and down. Doris flossed

between the teeth
with a string.
Grace sprayed blue
mouthwash into the
air. Then Frank,
the Caramel Clump
Bar, came on.

He sat right on top of Yoko's tooth box.

"I am stuck here
forever!" said Frank.

The lights went out. The spotlight went on.

The dentist came in. Claude pulled Caramel
Frank from the tooth with his dental
cleaning tool.

"This candy bar has made a terrible hole in
the tooth. Now I must drill it and fill it," said
Claude. *"Buzz Buzz."*

Suddenly from inside the cavity box came the most awful drilling noise.

ZIN ZIN ZIZZ ZIZZ WOWEEEEE Zeeeee!

Claude did not know what had happened.

The lights went on.

All the mamas and daddies clapped and cheered.

They asked for the drill again and again and one more time.

Everyone took a bow.

And Yoko came out fiddling!

Make New Friends

GOLDEN RULE THE SIXTH

Some people shine like a star in the first moment.
Others keep their light hidden until
they are ready to show us.

Tap, tap, tap!

"Attention, everybody!" Mrs. Jenkins said.

Mrs. Jenkins wrote a poem on the board.

"Can anyone read this?" she asked.

Yoko tried. Timothy tried.

"I can read it!" said Claude.

Claude tried. Everyone waited. But even

Claude could not read it.

"I will read it out loud!" said Mrs. Jenkins.

"Make new friends,

but keep the old.

One is silver and

the other is gold!"

"What does it mean, boys and girls?" asked Mrs. Jenkins.

"Tinfoil is silver," said Charles.

"The sunset is gold!" said Claude.

"Well," said Mrs. Jenkins, "that's true, Charles and Claude.

"Now, we have a special event today. A new classmate has moved to Hilltop School.

Her name is Juanita. She comes all the way from Texas."

"Is she big or little?" asked one of the Franks.

"Can she jump rope?" asked Charles.

"Why don't we ask her?" said Mrs. Jenkins.

"Here she is!"

Juanita's mother brought Juanita into Mrs. Jenkins's class.

Mrs. Jenkins played the "Welcome" song. Everybody sang it.

"Purple grow the violets!
Green grows the grass!
Here's a hearty welcome
to our kindergarten class!"

Juanita looked scared to pieces.

"Yoko, will you be the captain of the Friend Ship, for today?" asked Mrs. Jenkins.

"Yes," said Yoko.

Yoko took Juanita's hand out of Juanita's mother's hand.

She sat Juanita at the very next desk.

All morning, Juanita was too scared to say a word.

At lunchtime, everybody sang the "Clean Hands" song. Juanita did not know the words.

"I will teach you," said Yoko.

By mistake the Franks sat on Juanita's lunch.

"Don't worry," said Yoko. "I am the captain of the Friend Ship. That means I will take care of you!"

Yoko stood on Mrs. Jenkins's chair.

"Please, everybody, give something to Juanita
so that she has lunch," said Yoko.

Nora gave Juanita half her sandwich.

Charles gave his celery.

Grace gave Juanita her hard-boiled egg.

 Fritz gave his apple.

Doris made a squeeze-cheese

tower on a plate.

And the Franks offered up their franks

and beans.

Soon Juanita had enough for four lunches.

At playtime, Charles, Doris, and Fritz asked
Juanita if she could jump rope double Dutch.

"I'll watch," said Juanita.

Frank asked Juanita how long she could stand on one foot. "*I* can do it for a long time!" said Frank.

"Maybe I'll try it next time," said Juanita.

"What would *you* like to do, Juanita?" asked Yoko.

"Just sit and watch," said Juanita.

"That's what we'll do," said Yoko. "Because I am the captain of the Friend Ship!"

Yoko and Juanita watched Claude do backflips.

During snack time, Yoko taught Juanita the words to the "Snack Time" song.

"Too much to remember in one day!" said Juanita.

At school-bus time, everybody lined up for the bus.

"I have to wait for my mother," said Juanita. "I hope she does not get lost!" Juanita's voice squeaked.

"Don't cry," said Yoko. "I will wait with you, because I am the captain of the Friend Ship!" Juanita and Yoko waited in the classroom.

"I will go and call your mother, Yoko,"

said Mrs. Jenkins. "Then she will not worry."

Yoko took out her violin. She played
"Twinkle, Twinkle, Little Star" for Juanita,
so that Juanita would not cry.

"I wish I could do something wonderful like
that," said Juanita. "Everybody in Hilltop School
does something special.

"Charles jumps double Dutch.

"Frank stands on one foot.

"Claude can do backflips.

"You play beautiful music. But I don't do anything special," said Juanita.

"They must do lots of wonderful things in Texas," said Yoko.

"It's about the same in Texas," said Juanita. "We even have the same poem about silver and gold."

"Can you read that by yourself?" asked Yoko.

"Of course," said Juanita.

"Even Claude can't read that!" said Yoko.

"There is nothing to it!" said Juanita. "My sister is the Texas spelling-bee champion, and I know all her words!"

"That is pretty wonderful!" said Yoko.

"See you tomorrow!"